3/10 ✻writing noted on endpaper -MID

P9-DEU-721

j KIN   4/09
Kingfisher, Rupert.
Madame Pamplemousse and her
incredible edibles
32148001497774

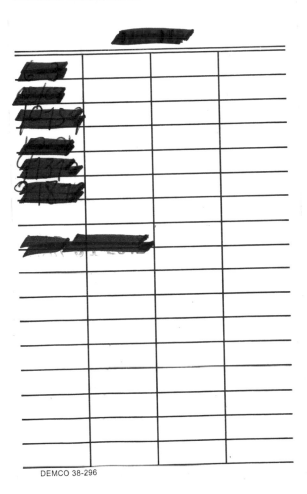

DEMCO 38-296

Madame Pamplemousse

AND HER

Incredible Edibles

3 2148 00149 7774

j
KIN

Madame Pamplemousse

AND HER

Incredible Edibles

Rupert Kingfisher

ILLUSTRATED BY

Sue Hellard

BLOOMSBURY
CHILDREN'S
BOOKS

NEW YORK • BERLIN • LONDON

Middletown Public Library
Middletown, RI 02842

4|09

Text copyright © 2008 by Rupert Kingfisher
Illustrations copyright © 2008 by Sue Hellard
All rights reserved. No part of this book may be used or reproduced
in any manner whatsoever without written permission from the publisher,
except in the case of brief quotations embodied in critical articles or reviews.

First published in Great Britain by Bloomsbury Publishing Plc
Published in the United States by Bloomsbury U.S.A. Children's Books
175 Fifth Avenue, New York, New York 10010

Library of Congress Cataloging-in-Publication Data
Kingfisher, Rupert.
Madame Pamplemousse and her incredible edibles / Rupert Kingfisher ;
illustrated by Sue Hellard. — 1st U.S. ed.
        p.   cm.
Summary: Forced to work in her unpleasant uncle's horrible restaurant,
a Parisian girl finds comfort and companionship in a shop nearby that sells otherworldly
foods prepared by a mysterious cook and her cat.
ISBN-13: 978-1-59990-306-4 • ISBN-10: 1-59990-306-7
[1. Food—Fiction. 2. Supernatural—Fiction. 3. Restaurants—Fiction.
4. Cooks—Fiction. 5. Paris (France)—Fiction. 6. France—Fiction.]
I. Hellard, Susan, ill. II. Title.
PZ7.K59Mad 2008   [Fic]—dc22   2008010409

First U.S. Edition 2008
Typeset by Dorchester Typesetting Group Ltd
Printed in the U.S.A. by Quebecor World Fairfield
2 4 6 8 10 9 7 5 3

All papers used by Bloomsbury U.S.A. are natural, recyclable products
made from wood grown in well-managed forests. The manufacturing processes
conform to the environmental regulations of the country of origin.

Chapter One

In the city of Paris, on the banks of the river, tucked away from the main street down a narrow, winding alley, there is a shop. A small, rather shabby-looking shop with faded paint-work, a dusty awning and dark, smoky windows. The sign above the door reads 'Edibles', as it is a food shop selling all kinds of rare and exotic delicacies. But they are not just rare and they are not just exotic, for this shop belongs to Madame Pamplemousse, and she sells the strangest, the rarest, the most delicious, the most extraordinary, the most incredible-tasting edibles in all the world.

Inside, the shop is cool and musty-smelling, lit only by candlelight. In the flickering shadows, great bunches of sausages and dried herbs, strings of garlic and chilli peppers, and giant salted meats hang from the ceiling. Rows of cheeses are laid out on beds of dark green leaves and all around there are shelves winding

up to the ceiling, crammed with bottles
and strangely shaped jars.

But look closer and you'll find these
aren't just plain sausages, they're
sausages of Bison and Black Pepper,
Wild Boar and Red Wine, and Minotaur
Salami with Sage and Wild Thyme. Among
the dried meats there are Salt-Cured Raptor
Tails, Pterodactyl Bacon, Smoked Sabre-
Toothed Tiger and Rolled Tyrannosaurus Rex
Tongue. The cheeses are of an unimaginable
smelliness, some dating back to medieval
times, and each of the pots and jars have their

contents written in fine, purple
letters: Scorpion Tails in Smoked
Garlic Oil, Crocodile Kidneys in

Blueberry Wine, Cobra Brains in Black
Butter, Roast Piranha with Raspberry Coulis,
Electric Eel Pâté with Garlic and
Prunes, Great White Shark Fin in
Banana Liquor and Giant Squid
Tentacle in Jasmine-Scented Jelly.

Underneath the shop, down a winding
spiral staircase, at the end of a long, dark
corridor, there is a door. A door that is
forever kept locked. For it is behind this
door that Madame Pamplemousse cooks her
rarest delicacy, a delicacy sold in the tiniest
little jar with a label upon which nothing is
written. The label is blank and the ingredients
are a secret, since it is the single most
delicious, the most extraordinary, the most

incredible-tasting edible of them all.

But even though Madame Pamplemousse sells the most delicious food ever tasted, her shop is by no means famous in the city of Paris. And nor would she ever want it to be. For she makes enough to get by and is happy each day to awake at dawn, drink a small black coffee and open up her shop, serving her customers and meeting with her suppliers. And come sundown she likes nothing better than to sit on her balcony above the rooftops with her cat, Camembert, discussing the day's events over a bottle of Violet-Petal Wine.

Camembert was a stray that had wandered in off the streets one night after a particularly vicious encounter with a pack of Siamese.

During the fight, Camembert had lost one of his eyes, but this was nothing compared to what happened to the Siamese.  Suffice it to say, he had since become known as a cat you don't mess with. From the first, he and Madame Pamplemousse had taken an instant liking to each other, and they lived together in perfect harmony, even though he would sometimes upset the customers by threatening to bite the ones he didn't like.

One person Camembert disliked intensely was a big pig-like man called Monsieur Lard. Lard ran a restaurant in the centre of the city – a big, flashy restaurant called the Squealing Pig. The problem with the restaurant was that although Lard thought his cooking some of the finest in Paris, it was, in fact, absolutely revolting. Whatever he cooked either turned out too greasy, or too sugary, or too fatty. The other problem was that Lard used to treat his customers in a way that was even greasier than his cuisine. On one occasion, to impress a Hollywood film star who had stopped by for a light lunch, he served up a whole baby lamb deep-fried in batter and smothered in orange syrup, which had the unfortunate conse-quence of making the film star violently sick.

Monsieur Lard had a team of chefs working in his kitchen, many of them excellent, but only a fool would dare criticise Lard's very own 'Specialities of the House'. For Lard's only real talent was to make people afraid of him. Experienced cooks, who had worked in some of the best and busiest kitchens in Paris, wobbled like jellies and began dropping things the moment Lard entered the room. Even the restaurant's Head Chef, once a talented cook, had been reduced to a quivering wreck after years of Lard's bullying and from being forced to prepare such revolting recipes as Pig's Ear Pizza, Kidney Burger with Double Cream, Offal and Seafood Sausages or Crab Ravioli in a Warm White Chocolate Sauce.

By far the best chef at the Squealing Pig was, in fact, Lard's niece, a girl called Madeleine. Madeleine was sent by her parents each summer to stay with her 'big jolly uncle'.

When she told them her
uncle was not really
jolly but a greedy, fat
bully, her mother
nearly fainted and her
father told her not to
be so selfish. So ever since,
while they went off on safari or a round-the-
world cruise, she would be sent to work in the
kitchens of the Squealing Pig. This usually
involved doing a lot of smiling. Lard was
obsessed with smiling. Everyone – the waiters,
the waitresses, the cooks and even the cleaners
behind the giant kitchen doors – was required
to smile at all times.

The restaurant actually did quite well from

rich tourists and passers-by, who assumed the food had to be good since it was so expensive. And apart from Lard's Specialities, it was all quite palatable. But this wasn't enough for Monsieur Lard. More than anything he wanted to become famous. He wanted to be recognised as a great chef.

Sadly for him, this wasn't going to happen. Probably because he was actually the worst chef the world had ever known. And the harder he tried, the more repulsive and ridiculous his cooking became. Until one day he made a remarkable discovery, and that discovery was due entirely to Madeleine, his niece.

Chapter Two

Apart from smiling, Madeleine's main job at the Squealing Pig was washing-up. An awful lot of washing-up. Despite being the best chef in the whole kitchen, she was never allowed to cook, under strict instructions from her uncle.

This was ever since the day she had made soup.

Madeleine had been cooking since she was quite young but had picked up a good deal from working in the kitchen. The soup was a deliciously light, lemony broth flavoured with fresh herbs. She had made it for her uncle in an effort to please him.

At first Monsieur Lard had devoured it greedily, spooning huge ladlefuls into his mouth so that dribbles ran down his chin. But as soon as he found out who cooked it, he paused mid-slurp, his face darkening.

'What's wrong, Uncle?' she said. 'Did I use too much lemon?'

Lard spat the remaining contents of his mouth on to the floor. 'Don't muck about in my kitchen!' he bellowed.

'But I wasn't mucking about, I promise! I cooked it for you specially!'

He chuckled, shaking his head. 'Don't be ridiculous,' he said. 'You can't cook!' And then he lifted up the entire soup cauldron and tipped it out of the window.

The truth was she had made him so violently jealous he would never allow her to go near a cooker again. So instead she had to scrub the plates, pots and pans – giant heaps of them stacked up to the ceiling and every one covered in slimy fat. As a special treat on Saturdays she might be allowed to clean out

the fridges instead or empty out the
bins. Or sometimes, if she was
very lucky, she might be sent
to fetch supplies.

One day, while checking
the stock cupboard, the Head
Chef found they were clean out of Mixed
Innards Pâté. This was a mixture of various
unnamed body parts of various unnamed ani-
mals, cured in fat and dyed bright pink.

No one liked it much except for Monsieur
Lard, but he was rather partial to it, so they
could not run out on pain of death. When the
Head Chef found the cupboard was bare he let
out a piercing scream. But Madeleine, seeing
her chance to escape the kitchen, offered to go

and fetch some more.

Usually this meant a trip to the nearby market, which was a straight walk down the riverbank. But Madeleine preferred the slightly longer route round the back streets. The Squealing Pig was in the city's busiest district, but the back led out into a maze of narrow lanes and winding alleys. At this time of day they were normally quiet, except for the occasional rat, but that didn't bother Madeleine. After all, they minded their own business just like her.

Strangely, this day she found the streets entirely empty of rats, but what she did see was a cat: a long white cat suddenly darting across her path. It scampered up ahead of her until it stopped at the end of the street.

She thought she recognised it. Sometimes, while washing dishes at night, she would see a white cat perched on the wall above the dust-bins. In the moonlight she had first mistaken it for an owl. Believing it to be the same one, she called out.

'Monsieur? Wait up, please, Monsieur . . .'

But it had already gone, disappearing round the corner. For some reason, she decided to follow it. Turning the corner herself, she came on to a steep, narrow lane running uphill. Above her, rows of washing were hanging between shuttered windows and wrought-iron balconies, and the afternoon sun shone bright on the white sheets.

At the top of the hill she found herself in a quiet, dusty cobbled street, mostly empty but for a shop. A small, rather shabby-looking shop. And there was the white cat, scurrying across the road. Then the most bizarre thing happened and Madeleine wondered if her eyes were playing tricks. For when the cat reached the shop, it appeared to rear up on its hind legs, open the front door and walk through it.

Creeping up to the window, Madeleine peered in, but it was so dark and smoky all she could see was the orange glow of candle flames. The door, however, was ajar, and so she went inside.

It took a moment for her to adjust to the

candlelight, but what she noticed first was the smell. A cool, musty odour, like the air in an old church – but one that was made entirely out of cheese. She could detect a deeper, spicier note beneath that was warm and exotic and reminded her of a Middle Eastern spice bazaar. But that was not all, for Madeleine had a highly developed nose; there was also a scent like lavender that has been drying in hot sunlight.

Then, suddenly, from out of the shadows a woman appeared. Madeleine nearly screamed.

'May I help you, Mademoiselle?' said Madame Pamplemousse.

'S-s-sorry, Madame,' said Madeleine, edging

towards the door. 'I was on my way to the market; I came in here by mistake . . .' And she made to go, when she was stopped by the woman's voice.

'What to buy, Mademoiselle?'

'Pâté, Madame.'

'Ah yes,' she said, 'I have just the thing.' And from below the counter she produced a small bottle con-taining a dark green substance. It had a label on which was written in fine, purple script:

Pâté of North Atlantic Sea Serpent
with Green Peppercorn Mustard

 Madeleine wasn't quite sure what to make of this. Many people might have taken it for a hoax or some kind of joke. Madeleine, however, never doubted it was made from genuine sea serpent; it was simply that this was not the kind of pâté she had been sent to buy.

'I'm sorry, Madame, but I think there's been some mistake.'

'You said pâté, Mademoiselle?'

'Yes, but –'

'That is the finest pâté currently available.'

'But I have such a small sum,' said Madeleine, showing her money. 'I couldn't possibly afford . . .' But before she could finish,

Madame Pamplemousse had already reached over and plucked the money from her hand. 'That will be quite sufficient, thank you.' And the next instant she was gone.

She did this so quickly it took Madeleine a couple of seconds to realise. But there was no mistaking it: the woman was nowhere to be seen and the shop had fallen silent.

Except that it wasn't silent. It struck Madeleine it had never been silent from the moment she had walked in. All around, in the shadows, there had been a patter of little noises, like gasps or tiny whispers, and a faint, persistent wheeze. Just then she heard a sudden growling and something slithering across the floor. Remembering the mention of sea serpents, Madeleine bolted straight out of the door.

Chapter Three

When the Head Chef found out that Madeleine had brought back the wrong sort of pâté, he burst into tears. He was badly afraid of Monsieur Lard as it was, but this was too much.

'He will slaughter us!' he cried. 'He will boil us alive!' He wailed inconsolably, burying his head in his hands.

Madeleine had to think quickly. He was probably right; her uncle would find out and his rage would be terrible. But then she remembered the extraordinary woman she had met in the shop, and the memory gave her an odd sort of courage.

She took a baguette, still warm from the oven, and carefully broke the seal of the jar containing the strange green substance. She spread some thinly on to a piece of bread and handed it to the Head Chef.

'Here,' she said. 'Eat this – it will make you feel better.'

The Head Chef was deaf to her in his misery. 'He will roast us in the oven, yes – but first he will smother us in goose fat –'

'Eat it!' she said sternly, and he did as he was told.

He took the bread, with tears still dripping down his nose, and bit into it cautiously. He chewed the morsel slowly around his mouth, frowning all the while, until suddenly his face froze rigid and his eyes opened very wide.

'Is it all right?' asked Madeleine anxiously, but he did not reply.

For it was like no food he

had ever tasted, nor like any taste he had ever experienced. The sensation was more as if he had actually become the sea serpent and was swimming through cool, dark waters. He turned to Madeleine, about to speak, when to his horror he saw the piggy eyes of Monsieur Lard staring at them through the kitchen doors.

'What's going on here?' said Lard darkly.

'Monsieur Lard! How n-nice to see you,' stammered the Head Chef and then went horribly blank, unable to think what to say next.

Madeleine cut in quickly. 'I hope you don't mind, Uncle,' she said. 'We were just doing some extra smiling practice.' The Head Chef nodded vigorously, and to prove it they both

grinned from ear to ear like a pair of mad hyenas. The Head Chef made what was probably intended as a laugh but came out as a whinnying cackle.

Monsieur Lard eyed them suspiciously while fingering his moustache. However, this appeared to satisfy him.

'Not bad,' he said. 'But could try harder.' He strode off, leaving the heavy steel doors swinging behind him.

Madeleine and the Head Chef took several deep breaths to stop their hearts from pounding. 'Don't worry,' whispered Madeleine. 'I'll replace it tomorrow, I promise.'

He began to cry quietly again. 'But if somebody orders pâté tonight, Mademoiselle?

Then we are lost!'

'But we can give them this,' she said, seiz-
ing the green jar.

'No, Mademoiselle!' he cried.

'Why? Is it not good?'

'Good?' he said. 'No, it's not *good*. It's not
good at all.' He paused, apparently overcome
with great emotion. 'It is superb! It is miraculous! Mademoiselle, you have there what is,
without question, the finest pâté ever tasted –
which is precisely why we cannot serve it
tonight, since nothing that delicious has ever
been served in this restaurant before.
Monsieur Lard will immediately smell a rat!'

Orders to the kitchen came through from
the restaurant via a machine that printed them

off for each table. The machine made a shrill, electric bleating sound as it produced each ticket. And there it was in black and white: at 7.30 that evening a table of seven had all ordered pâté for their first course.

The Head Chef was the first to see the order. He received the news remarkably calmly, tearing off the printed slip and taking it over to show Madeleine. Then he solemnly shook her hand.

'Mademoiselle,' he said, in a low voice, 'I want you to know that working with you has been a pleasure and that if I had to be cooked alongside somebody, I could not have chosen better company.'

'But can't we just try the new pâté?' she said. 'Maybe no one will notice.'

'Believe me, they'll notice!'

'But we have no choice!'

And then she began to cry a little. The Head Chef touched her lightly on the shoulder. 'Courage, Mademoiselle,' he said softly.

'Hey!' snapped a small, thin waiter who had come dancing into the kitchen. 'Get a move on with those pâtés!'

Hurriedly, Madeleine and the Head Chef spooned out the

contents of the jar. They handed the plates to the waiter, who managed to carry all seven of them, including one balanced on his head. At first they thought he hadn't noticed anything unusual, but then, just as he was about to leave the kitchen, he paused to raise an eyebrow. 'Funny colour, isn't it?' he said tartly and twirled elegantly out of the door.

The wait that followed was the most dreadful either Madeleine or the Head Chef had ever known. Normally, after a starter the waiter would come back and tell them when to begin preparing the next course. But this time, sinisterly, he did not. As the minutes ticked by, they began to suspect the worst.

But then a most peculiar thing happened. The table of seven asked for more.

They had been behaving strangely ever since receiving their first course. Until then they had been the noisiest customers in the restaurant, but since tasting the green pâté they had not said a word and did nothing but chew silently, staring into space.

Mixed Innards Pâté usually left people feeling so queasy they could barely finish what was on their plate. To order more was unheard of, and Monsieur Lard's suspicions were instantly raised. It didn't take long to find out who the culprit was either. He had several spies among his staff and one of them, the small, thin waiter who moved like a dancer, told Lard about the strangely coloured pâté. He also remarked, in passing, how he had seen Madeleine on her way into the city that morning.

Lard came thundering through the kitchen doors. The cooks were trying their best to conceal Madeleine inside a giant tin of vegetable oil, but Lard flung them aside.

He grabbed Madeleine by the shoulders and lifted her high in the air. 'Where did you get it?' he bellowed. 'WHERE DID YOU GET IT?'

He was shaking her so violently she could not reply, but then, from out of her pocket fell the tiny green jar, and it plummeted to the ground. The contents lay splattered every-where, but Monsieur Lard had his answer. For there, on a shard of broken glass, was a small piece of label, on which was written in fine, purple script:

Edibles
62 Rue d'Escargot

Rumours spread quickly throughout the city, and the next day customers began flocking to the Squealing Pig after they heard tell of the strange and delicious food Lard was serving there. Then, wonder of wonders, a table was booked by Monsieur Langoustine.

Monsieur Langoustine was a food critic, the most powerful food critic in Paris. A bad review from Langoustine and your restaurant  would close immediately. As Monsieur Langoustine never gave a good review, the best you could hope for was not to displease him too severely, and if this happened, your restaurant would be permanently booked out.

If Langoustine was coming, Lard would have to give him something very special. And that meant a visit to the Rue d'Escargot.

Chapter Four

Monsieur Lard made his way along
the riverbank, turning left down the
winding alleys that were hot and dusty in the
morning sun, and came through the doorway
into the dim, candlelit gloom. Instantly, his

nose was met by the scent of herbs and sweet spices and the deep, musty tang of old cheese. He wrinkled his nose. Something in the smell made him uneasy.

There was a small brass bell on the counter, which he hit once, and then again, as it appeared to make no sound. He drummed his fingers impatiently, casting his eyes around, when there was a sudden, fearsome screech and something leapt up out of the dark.

Lard stumbled back, nearly falling over in fright.

It was a cat – a thin white cat with a patch across one eye. It sprang down on to the

counter, where it scowled and bared its fangs. 'Mangy brute!' Lard grumbled. And then, from out of the shadows appeared a woman dressed in black.

'May I help you, Monsieur?' said Madame Pamplemousse.

Lard felt distinctly uncomfortable. The two of them had caught him completely off guard and there was something in her voice that he didn't like either. It sounded as if she knew what he was up to.

'Madame,' said Lard, grinning greasily, 'yesterday my niece came in here to buy some pâté. Of course, you will not remember –'

'I remember,' she said.

'Ah. Well, in that case, I'm sorry to inform

you she made a mistake. Foolishly, she only bought the one jar, while I had instructed her to buy ten.'

'That's a lot of pâté, Monsieur,' said Madame Pamplemousse after a pause.

'Aha, yes!' he chuckled, rubbing his hands. 'My dear little mother is coming to dinner tonight. A small woman but a big appetite.'

'Alas, Monsieur, I'm afraid it is impossible.'

'Very little is impossible where money is concerned, Madame. I'm sure we could come to an agreeable price.'

'Perhaps you did not read the label?' said Madame Pamplemousse. 'Sea serpents of the North Atlantic are something of a rarity. The last one is, I gather, currently somewhere in the fresh waters of Scotland. Your niece had my last jar. But perhaps I could interest Monsieur in something else?'

Lard felt a rage so power-ful he had to control it by smiling even wider. 'You obviously take me for a fool, Madame,' he said, laughing dangerously. 'Someone you can fob off with any old rubbish.'

'I assure you nothing in this shop is rubbish,' said Madame Pamplemousse coolly. The cat hissed and arched its back.

Monsieur Lard licked his fingers and then proceeded to count banknotes from his wallet.

'I am interested only in the best, Madame, you understand? The very best you've got.'

'The best, Monsieur?' she said, raising an eyebrow. Lard felt sweat break out on his fore-head. 'Very well,' she said. 'If that is what you wish, try this.' And in one swift motion she reached below the counter and brought up a tiny jar. It was no bigger than an eggcup, sealed in wax, with a rough, yellow paper label.

Lard took the jar suspiciously. It appeared to contain a kind of paste. Yes, that was it. But in the candlelight it changed colour. From one side it glowed a deep, golden red, the

colour of flames, and from another, soft lavender, and from another angle it shifted to aqua-
marine and then to sapphire blue.

'But what is this? I cannot read the label. It
looks like . . . why, it is blank, Madame.'

'That's because it has no name,' she said.

'No name? And no ingredients either?'

'The ingredients are a secret,' she said.
'However, I can assure you it will not
disappoint.'

Monsieur Lard wiped his brow. His prize
was now so near, if only he could manage to
control himself. His composure was not
helped by the cat, which was making a low
growling sound.

'But the jar is so small. If it is as good as you

say, perhaps you could sell me . . . ooh, I don't
know . . . a hundred jars?'

'Your mother must be hungry, Monsieur.'

Lard broke out into hysterical laughter. 'My
idea of a joke, Madame.'

But Madame Pamplemousse did not smile.
'The one jar is all I have at present. It is a fea-
ture of this particular delicacy that it cannot be
cooked to order. Any attempt to do so would
severely impair its flavour. However, a little
goes a long way and you will find more than

 enough there to feed a table of a
hundred. I think that should be
enough for Monsieur and his
. . . guest?'

Lard bowed his head. 'You are

too kind, Madame. Certainly, one jar will suffice. Now, we have not discussed a price . . .' Hurriedly, he began putting the money back into his wallet. 'Presumably, as it is so small, the price will be small as well?'

'Pay me nothing,' she said, 'until you have tried it. Then tomorrow come and give me whatever you think it's worth. But on one condition: serve it simply, as simply as possible, with nothing more than a good wine and  good bread. And now,' she clapped her hands, 'if that is all, good day, Monsieur.' And the next instant she was gone, vanishing into the darkness.

Chapter Five

Back at the Squealing Pig, everyone was smiling. Monsieur Lard was patrolling the kitchen and the preparations for the evening were being supervised to the last detail. He had followed Madame

Pamplemousse's instructions and served the strangely coloured paste unaccompanied except by bread, but he could not resist putting a small pig's ear garnish beside it on every plate.

Ever since the night of the Sea Serpent Pâté, Monsieur Lard had been watching Madeleine suspiciously. She had, of course, been the one responsible for his strange turn of fortunes, but to Monsieur Lard this made her danger-ous. Because she knew he was a fraud – that he was serving someone else's cooking and pretending it was his own.

It was now strictly forbidden for anyone to speak to her. As a result, a strange cloud of suspicion formed around Madeleine, and it wasn't just Monsieur Lard but the whole staff who began treating her differently. People avoided speaking to her; waiters would no longer stack their dishes but would dump them straight in the sink, splashing her with greasy water. And when it came time for the staff meal, she found herself mysteriously left out. It was only her friend, the Head Chef, who, at immense personal risk, made sure that she was fed.

Outside the restaurant, a great queue of people had formed along the riverbank. The mood was that of a street party, the evening air buzzing with excited chatter. News of Monsieur Langoustine's arrival had spread quickly throughout Paris and there was a great burst of applause as a black limousine pulled up and the black-suited chauffeur got out to open the passenger door to reveal Monsieur Langoustine, dressed in his customary black. Two of Lard's waiters escorted the critic to his table and, as soon as he was seated, glasses of pink champagne and pink jewel-encrusted plates bearing Madame Pamplemousse's delicacy were brought out and served to everyone. The diners were still chattering away and drinking wine when they first tasted it. And then they all fell silent.

The crowds of people queuing up around the corner became silent as well, surprised by this sudden, eerie hush. For each and every one of the diners had stopped talking at the same instant and were now gazing into the distance with a strange look on their faces.

In the kitchen, they all ceased what they were doing and went to the window to look. People passing in the nearby streets stopped to stare, to see what everyone else was staring at, and they too fell silent. Cars driving past came to a halt as drivers got out to find out what was going on, and soon the entire city of Paris had stopped still and was waiting to see what would happen, and for a long while you could hear nothing but the sound of the wind, rustling in the trees. But then a grand old chef who was 115 years old stopped chewing, swallowed and stood up.

'Ah yes,' he said, 'now I understand.' And then he sat down again and died immediately, but with a look of great joy on his face. And then the diners all began to cheer as one. People were laughing, singing and dancing; some wept, others proposed marriage to who-ever was sitting next to them.

From a balcony high above the rooftops, Camembert growled. He and Madame Pamplemousse were sharing a bottle of Rose-Petal Wine.

'Monsieur Lard is a fat, thieving pig!' Camembert spat out each word. 'He will become rich, he will become famous. And all because of you!'

Madame Pamplemousse puffed on her pipe.

'Look down there,' she said. 'Tonight, people are happy. They are laughing, singing; they feel anything is possible and, yes, it's because of my cooking. I'm happy for them. But to have the whole of Paris on my doorstep, demanding more . . .' She shrugged. 'It is not for me. Monsieur Lard is welcome to it.'

'I tell you what,' said Camembert, scowling with his one eye. 'I'll kill him.'

She shook her head.

'It's no trouble,' he said. 'It would be my pleasure.'

'There's no need. Besides,' she said, 'the

recipe works in mysterious ways; you never know quite what might happen. Now be a good cat,' and she waved him gently away. 'I want to enjoy the sunset in peace.'

So Camembert snarled and stalked off to a high rooftop, where he was to meet his girl-friend, Chanterelle. She at least would show him sympathy.

Chapter Six

As Madame Pamplemousse predicted, the press beat a path to Lard's door. He appeared on the cover of *Paris Match* and was interviewed on national television. To everyone's amazement, the other guest in the studio was Monsieur Langoustine, who absolutely never gave interviews. The presenter asked Langoustine what was so special about Lard's cooking.

At first, the food critic did not reply. The presenter waited eagerly, for in Paris Langoustine was revered as a philosopher, a guru and a mystic. When he finally spoke, the presenter was alarmed to hear a soft, piping voice that sounded more like a flute or a recorder than a human being.

'Well, well,' said Langoustine. 'Monsieur Lard must be very clever, for you ask me what is so special about his food. At first I would have said *nothing*.' He shrugged. 'On the face of it, Lard's restaurant is just like any other, if

rather more revoltingly furnished. Paris is, unfortunately, full of such places – fit to burst, you might say.' The presenter laughed politely. Langoustine stared at him a while before continuing.

'But then I tried Monsieur Lard's cooking and . . . *ooh la la!* I think to myself, what is this mysterious flavour? What is this miraculous taste? So it seems Monsieur Lard has a secret. A very big secret. Some kind of *ingredient X*.' Langoustine turned to Monsieur Lard slowly, making him squirm in his seat. 'I wonder what it could be.'

'That's the secret the whole of Paris is

trying to crack,' said the presenter. 'Monsieur Lard, do you have any plans to give it away?'

Monsieur Lard gave a hollow-sounding laugh. 'You want to know what it is? This secret, this ingredient X?' He paused for effect and then tapped his skull. 'It's right here,' he said.

But for Lard the awful truth was that he was as much in the dark as anyone else about this mysterious ingredient. Because the recipe didn't belong to him at all; it belonged to Madame Pamplemousse. And he was not about to let her keep it.

Chapter Seven

The next morning Lard woke after a troubled sleep. He had been having nightmares about Monsieur Langoustine with long pincers instead of arms, interrogating him in a cave beneath the sea. At one terrible moment Langoustine had removed his dark glasses to reveal . . . but then he had woken up.

Afterwards Lard was more than usually sweaty, so he lathered his armpits in powerfully scented soap and coated himself in aftershave. Then he put on one of his finest  mint-green-and-pink-striped suits and oiled his moustache. Monsieur Lard had a plan.

It was so beautifully simple. He kicked himself for not having thought of it before. When he had been in the shop, Madame Pamplemousse had been alone. She had that wretched cat, of course, but no assistant. Clearly she was too poor to afford one. So how could she refuse a sweet, charming girl with a dear smile who would work there for free? In other words, he would volunteer Madeleine for the job. Then, once inside, she could become his spy.

When he had finished oiling his moustache, Lard crashed into Madeleine's bedroom, singing 'What a beautiful morning!' at the top of his voice and tap dancing so that the floor shook. Then he yanked her out of bed and told her to start practising her smile. He also made her put on a ridiculous pink fairy outfit with silver wings.

'You don't fool me,' he said over breakfast. This consisted of a large fatty piece of bacon that had been boiled until it was grey. 'It's

always the quiet ones. You might look nice and polite on the outside, but I know you're really a little sneak underneath!'

He chuckled in a way that instantly gave her stomach ache. This was before she had even attempted the bacon, which was very gristly and difficult to cut into.

'But I'm giving you a chance to redeem yourself, a chance to put your sneaky little ways to good use!'

He brought his shiny, sweaty face up close.

'You're going back to that shop and you're

going to work for that woman as her assistant. And you'd better do as she says because she's not a big softy like me; one foot wrong and she'll chop you up for sausage meat!'

Madeleine remembered the eerie darkness of the shop and the mysterious woman in black appearing out of nowhere. The awful thing was, her uncle was right: she did feel like a sneak, because he was serving food from this woman's shop and passing it off as his own. And it was all Madeleine's fault; she had been the one who started it. Goodness knows what the woman would do to her if she found out.

'I want you to keep your eyes open. There's one special delicacy. One with no name, no ingredients on the label. I want you to find out how she makes it, what goes into it, right down to the last pinch of salt, do you understand me?'

'Yes, Uncle,' she said very faintly.

'Good girl!' He gave her an affectionate pinch on the cheek. 'And don't forget to smile!'

Monsieur Lard kept a tight grip on his niece's hand as he dragged her along the riverbank. Passers-by, seeing a big man holding hands with a small girl in a fairy costume, smiled at such a heart-warming sight. Eventually they turned down the winding little alley that led into the narrow cobbled

 street. And there was the shop.

They found the door was open and went inside. It took a while for them to adjust to the candlelight, but the shop appeared to be empty. Monsieur Lard rang the bell on the counter, but it was silent, so he rang it again several times.

'I trust last night went well, Monsieur?'

The voice came out of the darkness, making Lard cry out in shock. But the next moment there was the woman, standing right in front of him.

'Madame!' he sang in his oiliest voice. 'How nice to see you again and, if I may say, how

well you look. But last night! Such a delight-
ful evening; my mother simply adored your
little recipe.'

'I'm so glad she enjoyed it.'

'Enjoyed it? She scoffed the lot! But you
asked me to pay you whatever I deemed it
worth. So may I present this girl.'

Madame Pamplemousse stared at Madeleine.

'This is your payment, Monsieur?'

'Why yes, Madame. This is my niece,
Madeleine.'

'I'm not sure I understand. Are you pro-
posing I cook her as a rare delicacy?'

At this Madeleine's blood ran cold, but her
uncle roared with laughter. 'If you so wish,
Madame. I had in mind a little helper. She can

cook, she can clean, she can make your shop look brand-new.'

'As you may have noticed, Monsieur,' said Madame Pamplemousse, 'my shop has never looked "brand-new", nor do I think it ever will.'

'Come, come, let's be frank,' said Lard. 'You

are not a rich lady; you can afford no staff. Just think how useful she could be. After all, we know what a menace rats can be in this district.'

'We have no problem

with rats,' she said and, from a dark corner, Camembert burped loudly and licked his whiskers.

Lard's bull-like neck flexed itself horribly. He had to suppress a powerful urge to smash the whole place to pieces. But instead, he smiled. 'It may interest you to know I have recently made friends with many powerful people in television and the government.' His smile became greasier. 'They tell me how easily a shop like yours may be closed on the slightest suspicion of poor hygiene.'

To this Madame Pamplemousse did not immediately reply. Madeleine couldn't be sure but sensed that she was turning something over in her mind – that she was making some kind of decision. Then, with an awful feeling like someone squeezing a lemon inside her stomach, she realised Madame Pamplemousse was staring at her again. Madeleine steeled herself and, cautiously, stared back.

Madame Pamplemousse had the strangest eyes she had ever seen. They were a very deep purpley blue, the colour of wild lavender. By no means were they unpleasant eyes, nor were they unkind, but they weren't exactly kind either. Then, miraculously, she smiled. 'Very well, Monsieur,' she said. 'Since you make me such a charming offer, I accept.
She may indeed prove useful.'

Monsieur Lard beamed

with satisfaction. 'An excellent decision, Madame. She won't let you down, will you, Madeleine?'

'Of course not, Uncle,' said Madeleine.

'Any monkey business, you come straight to me.' Lard punched his hand for emphasis. 'I'll soon sort her out.'

'Thank you, Monsieur, that won't be necessary,' said Madame Pamplemousse curtly.

'You don't believe me, Madame?' Lard moved closer until his hulking body towered above her. 'I may look like a gentle man but I've still got one or two tricks up my sleeve.'

From high above Lard's head there was a tiny sound, such as of a stopper or cork being released from a bottle. A moment later, Lard

felt drops of moisture spot-
ting on his head.

'Arghh!' he cried.
'Even your confounded
roof is leaking!'

'Alas no, Monsieur,' said
Madame Pamplemousse. 'It is not my roof that
is leaking, but for some mysterious reason a
bottle has upturned itself on the highest shelf
and is dripping on to your head. Unfortunately
it is a bottle containing concentrated oil from
the Green Demon Pimento: a small but
extraordinarily powerful chilli that used to
grow in ancient Peru and was once worshipped
as a god by the Incas. It is so powerful that one
single drop is stronger than the hottest curry

in the world. I regret to inform you, Monsieur, that several drops appear to have landed on your head.'

But before she had finished, Lard's nostrils had already started to steam; his eyes went a bright green colour and he ran straight for the door, bellowing loudly like a bull. Then, as mysteriously as it had begun, the dripping stopped and, staring up, Madeleine thought she saw the darting shape of a long white body slipping behind the bottles on the highest shelf. Then all was silent and, looking down again, Madeleine realised she was alone.

Chapter Eight

Madame Pamplemousse and her cat had completely vanished. Madeleine had only looked up for a second; how could they have disappeared so quickly? She opened her mouth to call out but then thought better of it.

It might be some kind of trick they were playing. Perhaps they already suspected she was a spy. She shivered at the thought.

But not just that; there was something distinctly creepy about the place. It was partly the shadows made by the candle flames, which were long and spindly and danced across the walls, and the foods themselves, which seemed almost to be alive, as if the cheeses were softly sighing and the bunches of sausages whispering in their dry, garlicky voices.

As Madeleine's eyes grew accustomed to the gloom, she stared closer at the shelves. Each one was packed densely with shining coloured-glass containers and behind each row there would be another and another, as far as

the eye could see, and the shelves
themselves were all stacked
higgledy-piggledy up to the
ceiling. One was filled with
different types of mustard
in many shades of yellow.

Above this there was a dark, cavernous shelf
reaching into the shadows, and it was only
after she had counted back Olives, Black
Truffles, Caviar, Pickled Walnuts from the
Fourteenth Century, Woodland Snails Stuffed
with Sausage Meat, Python Heads with
Liquorice and Giant-Squid Eyes in Balsamic
Vinegar that she realised everything on it was
completely black.

Stepping back a couple of paces, she looked

up at another shelf and saw how all the bottles and jars were in varying shades of green.

Madeleine found an old, rickety ladder and, climbing up, she surveyed the winding tower of shelves about her and saw how they formed a carousel of moving colours, each one seeping into the other, blending subtly so that no one ever clashed or made itself too bold but shifted gracefully: from the golden hues of Barracuda Fillets in Garlic Butter to the dark, orchard greens of Grasshoppers in Tarragon Oil; from the rich purple of Lavender-Crusted Frogs' Legs to the dark crimson of Velociraptor Heart in Red Wine. And there, right at the top, on the highest shelf, was a tiny jar into which all the spinning hues were coiling and flickering, like flames reflecting in the glass.

She knew instinctively what it must be: it was the special delicacy for which her uncle wanted the recipe. Perhaps this jar would hold the secret. It might even have the ingredients on its label. She felt a sudden, overwhelming desire to snatch it and run away. Then she could give it to her uncle and it would all be over; she would be free.

Without stopping to think, she reached up.

And immediately regretted it. The ladder was not quite high enough and began to wobble. Desperately she tried to steady herself, just managing to get a hold when above her she heard a hissing sound, and there was Camembert on the highest shelf.

Madeleine screamed and let go her hand. The ladder tottered in mid-air for a second before plummeting straight to the ground.

And there, perfectly positioned at the precise point at which Madeleine would have landed, was Madame Pamplemousse, who caught her just in time. In fact, she caught the silver fairy wings, which meant they broke off from the back of Madeleine's dress, leaving her to fall only a small distance to the floor.

'So, Mademoiselle, you have found your way around?'

'Yes, Madame,' said Madeleine, somewhat shaken.

'You have a keen eye, I see. Very good. I am also delighted that you have lost those ridiculous wings. All in all, a most promising start.'

'Thank you, Madame,' said Madeleine.

 'Never mind Camembert. He makes no effort to put people at their ease. That's how he is; there's nothing I can do about it. Besides, he may have thought you were spying.'

Madeleine started when she heard this and began to go bright red. Quickly she averted her eyes. But when she looked up again, Madame Pamplemousse appeared not to have noticed. Instead, she was busy by the cheese counter, unwrapping a giant goat's cheese from an enormous green leaf. 'Well, Mademoiselle,' she said. 'Are you ready?'

And from that moment Madeleine began officially to be Madame Pamplemousse's assistant. Starting with the goat's cheese, she was taught about all 653 different varieties of cheese that were available in the shop. This included a mouldy blue cheese that dated back to the French Revolution and a soft, gooey ooze with a brownish green rind that was once a favourite of Joan of Arc. This was so unspeakably stinky that it had to be protected by a heavy marble lid several centimetres

thick, but even so Madeleine  was sure she sometimes saw it rattling and, on one occa-sion, heard it softly belch.

At the back of the shop there was a low doorway which led into an anteroom: a small kitchen area with a stone floor and a large, dark wooden table. It was here that she would be put to work each day, learning how to fillet an anchovy and to dress it in oils and spices, how to smoke an eel, how to make pâté from a sea serpent and how to squeeze the nectar from a violet.

Madame Pamplemousse would give precise but rather minimal instructions in the kitchen, and Madeleine discovered that someone who

did a lot of the actual cooking was Camembert. He
was, for example, particularly skilful with a whisk.

Via a set of steps, he would reach
the table on his hind legs, and then, with one
paw, whizz things together with astonishing
speed. Equally, when it came to chopping he
was incredibly fast. Madeleine could chop
quite fast herself but she was wary of some of
the knives, which looked like they might slice
off your finger before you had even noticed.
Though if ever she slowed down, Camembert
would scowl disdainfully and 'tsk' until she
speeded up.

But despite being afraid of them, Madeleine

found she rather liked Madame Pamplemousse and her cat. However frightening they might seem, at least they never bullied her or shouted at her. And each day when she arrived, the shop would be empty, but on the counter a small brass pot of hot chocolate would be waiting, at just the right temperature. And with the door open to the sunlit street outside, she would sit sipping this in the cool of the morning.

For as long as she had been at the Squealing Pig, Madeleine used to wake up every day wishing she could go back to sleep. But now she could hardly wait to get out of bed. The

tasks she was given at the
shop were getting much
more complex, though
strangely she found
she had to think less
about what she was
doing. Her instincts
seemed to be quickening and becoming more
refined.

Madame Pamplemousse had evidently
noticed this because she began to treat her differently: less like a child and more like an
equal – with respect. A respect, thought
Madeleine guiltily, she would soon repay by
betraying her.

By day she tried to forget about it, but come

sundown her heart would sink at the prospect
of her uncle's interrogation. For she had been
there two weeks now and still there was no
sight of the precious recipe.

At the back of the shop, in the far corner of
the little kitchen, there was a wrought-iron
spiral staircase winding down to the floor
below. Once, Madeleine had tiptoed down a
couple of flights and seen at the bottom a
corridor which led to a door. And she knew
it was behind that door that Madame
Pamplemousse cooked her most incredible
edible.

Chapter Nine

Monsieur Lard was getting desperate. The restaurant had been closed for well over a week and there was no question of reopening until he had the secret recipe. But by now the whole of Paris was clamouring for

tables, including the President of France himself, and Monsieur Lard had been forced to turn him down.

He was also growing suspicious, noticing how his niece had been looking a good deal happier lately.

'Having fun, eh? Getting on with your new friends? Well, don't worry, we'll soon have you back. There's a big pile of greasy plates in the kitchen and it's got your name on it.'

He smiled, beginning to enjoy himself again. He realised he had been missing Madeleine; he'd forgotten how much fun it was making her life a misery.

'I'm giving you one day. One more day. If I don't have the recipe by then, I will personally see to it that Madame Pamplemousse's shop is closed. I will ruin her just like that!' And he snapped his fat pink fingers.

The next morning, Madeleine awoke feeling sick. It wasn't just that she liked Madame Pamplemousse and didn't want to betray her. It was also that she was downright scared of her and even more so of Camembert. Worst of all, she had the dreadful feeling the whole thing had been her fault, right from the start.

She knew her uncle had made powerful friends. Even now he was in dialogue with an international food conglomerate, called simply 'FOOD', who were making offers for the

recipe in the region of 100 million euros.
With money like that, he could do pretty
much whatever he wanted.

Madeleine dreaded to think what would
happen if her uncle didn't get hold of the
recipe but suspected that ruining Madame
Pamplemousse would be the least of it. She
could not allow that. With great reluctance,
Madeleine decided what she must do.

It was while hunting for some Blue Rose-
Petal Jam the week before that she had found
something hidden beneath the shelves. She
had come across a row of dusty old
bottles containing Prehistoric
Fungus in Jurassic Vinegar that
appeared not to have been

touched in many years. By chance she knocked one of these out of its place and, after the cloud of dust had disappeared, she saw a small chink of light beneath it. Light from a downstairs room.

Just then she had heard a soft padding of feet on the spiral staircase below and, fearing Camembert, she had replaced the bottle hastily before she could be caught.

Now she knew she had no alternative. She must choose her moment carefully, wait until she was alone and then find her way back to that small chink of light.

As luck would have it, the morning after Lard gave his ultimatum, Madame Pamplemousse said she would be downstairs cooking all day, and asked Madeleine to look after the shop by herself. Camembert skulked about, keeping his eye on her, but when he saw she wasn't doing any harm he padded off down to the basement.

This was her moment. Now or never. Madeleine waited a good half-hour to make sure neither of them came back, and then, steeling herself, she crawled under the shelves. Very slowly and carefully she lifted up one of the bottles. She did this painstakingly with her fingertips so as to make no sound, but somehow the bottles still managed to clink together. They were made of old glass and gave off a soft but resounding chime. Madeleine froze, the bottle suspended in her hand, waiting to see if she had been overheard.

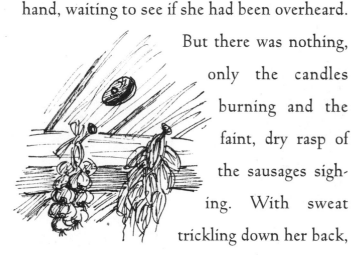

But there was nothing, only the candles burning and the faint, dry rasp of the sausages sigh-ing. With sweat trickling down her back, she lifted the bottle clear; and there it was, a hole in the floorboards. Putting her head down, she looked through this hole and found herself staring into a room.

It was a bare, mostly empty room, save for a stone fireplace and an old, wrought-iron cooker. In the centre of the room there was a long wooden table, with a chopping board on top of

it and a selection of rather cruel-looking
knives. There was no doubt about it. This was
the hidden kitchen, the room behind the
locked door.

Just then her heart
jumped, for a dark shape
suddenly flashed across the
floor beneath her. It was
Madame Pamplemousse!
Madeleine tried to control
her breathing and the
thumping in her chest,
which she thought must be

terribly loud. But Madame Pamplemousse
appeared not to have noticed and continued to
move about the kitchen at her rapid pace.

She had emerged from
under an archway, which
Madeleine presumed led
into the cavernous store-
rooms that lay beneath the
shop. Madame Pamplemousse kept disappear-
ing into the tunnel and then returning,
bearing ever more bizarre-looking items in her
arms.

She placed some of these on the chopping
board and then Camembert, holding an enormous meat cleaver in his paw, proceeded to
chop them into tiny pieces.

Meanwhile, Madame Pamplemousse was
mixing ingredients into a bowl, a dash of
something here, a pinch of something there,

all performed with immense speed and delicacy. During this the cat and his mistress never spoke but worked together as one, like musicians in perfect harmony.

Madeleine was straining to see which ingredients they were using, trying to put together the recipe in her head, but they were working so fast it was impossible to keep up. As soon as one of them finished chopping or spooning something from a jar, it went straight into the bowl and immediately they were reaching for the next ingredient. Until suddenly they stopped.

Stopped dead still. Madeleine held her breath but didn't know how long she could bear to and hoped very much the two of them would start cooking again. But they didn't. Instead, Madame Pamplemousse looked up, stared directly at Madeleine through the gap in the floorboards and said, 'Why don't you come down, Mademoiselle? You might be able to see better.'

Madeleine jumped up from the floor, banging her head on the shelf above her. She scrambled out as quickly as she could and made a dash for the open door. But her path was blocked. For in an astounding display of athleticism, Camembert had bounded up the spiral staircase, swung himself from a hanging bunch of thyme and landed dead in front of her, his claws outstretched.

Madeleine knew she was doomed. Trembling, she obeyed as Camembert marched her downstairs, down the winding stairwell, along the dark corridor and into the underground kitchen. When she saw Madame Pamplemousse, all she could do was throw herself at her mercy. This she regretted immediately as the stone floor was very hard and she bruised both her knees in the process.

'I'm so sorry!' she cried. 'I only did it to save you! My uncle said he would destroy you. He said if I didn't give him the recipe, he would ruin you just like that!' And she clicked her fingers.

Madeleine bowed her head low, waiting for her punishment. She felt certain it would be terrible, but also strangely relieved to have at last confessed her guilt. And so she waited.

And waited.

And then Madame Pamplemousse laughed.

'My dear Madeleine,' she said, 'let me first of all assure you that neither of us blames you. We know about your uncle and his ridiculous plan; there's little that escapes Camembert's eye. As a matter of fact, I think you are rather brave for attempting to spy on us.'

Camembert growled like a tiger, ready to pounce. 'Be quiet!' Madame Pamplemousse said sharply. Camembert tossed his head back and began licking his fur. 'Your uncle wishes to steal something from me: the recipe for The Most Incredible Edible Ever Tasted. Well, here it is.' And she promptly handed Madeleine a piece of yellow paper with a list written in purple ink.

Madeleine took the page and studied it closely. 'But I don't understand,' she said. 'Is that all?' For the incredible thing about the list was that none of the ingredients were in the least bit incredible. Some were quite rare but easily available in a city like Paris.

'Oh yes, that's all there is to it. I used to make it with Giant-Squid Stock, but there were no squids to hand one summer so I had to do without. A small improvement.'

'But if you give him the recipe . . .'

Madeleine's voice shook, 'then . . . he's won, hasn't he?'

Madame Pamplemousse smiled. 'Your uncle is a fool. He wishes to steal The Most Incredible Edible Ever Tasted and he thinks this is a simple matter of acquiring the recipe and . . .' here her lips pursed and Madeleine thought she was about to spit, 'copying it!'

Camembert spat for her, a great fur ball that landed at Madeleine's feet.

'The delicacy cannot be stolen, for it is made by my own hand, assisted by my colleague Camembert. The ingredients I use are not especially remarkable. Exquisite, yes, and delicious, but only things. It is you yourself that gives flavour to your cooking – your character, your dreams, your smiles, your tears. Your uncle is a bully. That is how his cooking will always taste. I may give your uncle the recipe, but Lard's customers should be warned: they might not like what they receive.'

Meanwhile, Camembert had gone back to chopping ingredients and was now  heating them over a low flame. He took a spoonful of this and raised it to Madame Pamplemousse's lips. She tasted it, then shook her head once. Camembert added some more spice, a pinch of something yellow and a pinch of something red.

Seeing them so engrossed, Madeleine thought it time to excuse herself as best she could. 'Is that all, then, Madame?' she asked quietly.

Madame Pamplemousse was concentrating on the pot which was cooking on the stove. She glanced up. 'Mm? Oh yes, thank you so much, Mademoiselle, that will be all.'

'Goodbye, then, Madame,' said Madeleine.

'Goodbye, Mademoiselle,' she said.

Madeleine waited a second or two to see if she might say more. But Madame Pamplemousse said nothing and so she made to leave.

'Oh . . . just one thing,' said Madame Pamplemousse as Madeleine reached the door. 'I thought you might like to try this before you go.' And she handed her a small piece of bread on which was spread some of the contents of the pot. By now it was starting to cool and as it did so it changed colour. When Madeleine took the bread from Madame Pamplemousse's hand it was a pale, mossy green, but before her eyes it shifted. At first it was a dark, warm red, the colour of burning coals, then a honey yellow, then the vivid blue of a peacock's tail, before finally resting on lavender: a deep purplish hue.

'It's ready now,' said Madame Pamplemousse and in her eyes there was a sudden flickering of a similar purple shade.

Afterwards, Madeleine would think back to that moment and try to remember when she first tasted it. But she could not, because tasting it was itself like a memory – all the best memories she had ever had suddenly sweeping through her like a gust of clear air. The flavours themselves, so light yet intense, subtle yet refreshing, seemed to wake her from a sleep. And all that time she had spent being afraid – doing her uncle's dirty work, acting as his spy – now seemed so far away, as if it belonged to a different person. Not that she

felt different; it was rather that she now
felt more completely herself.
And she realised then how,
more than anything, she loved
to cook. She had lost that
somewhere in the Squealing Pig, thanks to her
uncle, who made cookery seem so depressing.
Monsieur Lard only wanted to become
famous, to make the whole world love him.
She loved cooking for its own sake, the way
you loved another person.

'That is now yours to keep for ever.'
Madeleine's eyes had been closed but they
opened to find Madame Pamplemousse
smiling at her. 'No one can take that away.'

'But can I . . . can I really . . . ?' Madeleine

found herself barely able to speak.

'Can you cook? Why naturally,' said Madame Pamplemousse. 'Not only that, you have a talent, Mademoiselle. An exceptional talent. I knew it the instant we met.'

'But how, Madame?'

'Because you are one of us,' said Madame Pamplemousse. 'And people like us should stick together. My recipe affects people in different ways. Some dance, others sing. It reminded you who you are, that is all.'

'That's incredible,' said Madeleine.

'Naturally. That's why it's The Most Incredible Edible Ever Tasted. Now, we don't have much time. Your uncle is waiting for his recipe. Let's give him what he wants. Then tomorrow night he will serve it to his customers. But first it is time for you to invent a recipe of your own. Serve that tomorrow for the second course, and we shall see which they prefer. Come, let us get to work.'

And so they did, throughout the night, Madeleine starting at first hesitantly, then more confidently, to mix ingredients together.  She had long suspected that snails, liquorice, bay leaves and sorrel would make a good basis for a stock. These she slowly cooked until they had reached a good sludgy consistency, then she began adding other ingredients. She

 found she didn't have to think too hard about what to include; her wits were now sharper than ever, and she knew instinctively how a pinch of spice, a grind of pepper or a grating of zest would combine to produce the perfect flavour. Her hands played lightly over the shelves, all the while aided and assisted by Madame Pamplemousse and her cat (or actually just by Madame Pamplemousse, since Camembert did nothing but lick his fur), until, at last, she had produced her very own edible. To celebrate, the three of them took breakfast on Madame Pamplemousse's high balcony and toasted each other with hot chocolate as dawn was breaking over the city below.

Madeleine was ready. In her hands she bore the two recipes: the list of ingredients for The Most Incredible Edible and for her own unique creation. Then Madame Pamplemousse wished her good luck and Camembert offered to escort her along the riverbank, through the misty morning streets, back to the Squealing Pig.

Chapter Ten

When the news went out that the restaurant was opening again, the phone never stopped ringing. By now, only the wealthiest citizens of Paris were able to afford a table, but even so, the tables were by invitation only. The head of the FOOD Corporation had ordered his private jet to spin round in mid-flight when he got the news. The President of France had a special body double take over engagements so that he might attend.

By eight o'clock that morning, all of Lard's cooking staff had been despatched to buy the necessary ingredients. Lard was amazed by the recipe's simplicity.

'You mean that's it? There's nothing else to it?'

'Just what's on the list, Uncle,' said Madeleine.

'But surely some extra butter, a drizzle of double cream?'

'Just what's on the list,' she repeated.

'Well, I never!' said Lard. 'And there it was all this time, right under my very nose!' And he went off muttering to himself, occasionally lashing out to punch a wall or smash a piece of furniture.

By midday all of the ingredients had been bought, chopped, filleted, sliced, crushed and blended as dictated, to the letter, in the recipe. Smiling practice began soon after and work had to stop for a good two hours. Seeing her chance, Madeleine slipped away.

As quickly as she could, she took a saucepan and began to prepare the stock, just as she had done the night before in Madame Pamplemousse's kitchen. But the freedom she had felt there now abandoned her and in its place came a little, creeping fear. A fear that her recipe was no good – that it would backfire horribly and her uncle would be triumphant after all. But then the first delicate threads of steam rose up from the cooking pot to curl about her nostrils, and in that instant she forgot her fear. A new, coolly detached part of herself took hold, no longer rushing, but allowing the recipe to take shape at its own pace and natural rhythm.

Then, when it was done, she removed the saucepan from the heat and let it cool in a special hiding place in one of the store cupboards. This she man- aged just in time before a great stampede of chefs, forced to stop work during smiling practice, came charging through the kitchen doors.

By seven o'clock huge crowds had formed 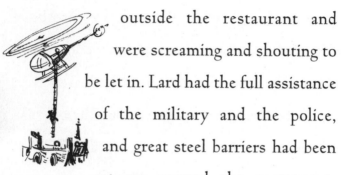 outside the restaurant and were screaming and shouting to be let in. Lard had the full assistance of the military and the police, and great steel barriers had been set up around the restaurant, patrolled by armed guards. Television crews were filming all the commotion and the crowd became hysterical when a helicopter appeared overhead, hovered above the restaurant, and a rope ladder dropped down. A bald, faceless man in a grey suit, who was the President of

France, climbed out of the helicopter, closely followed by a small, withered-looking man, who was the head of the FOOD Corporation.

It was more than Monsieur Lard could ever have dreamed of and he stepped out to meet the crowd, resplendent in his new pink and diamond-spangled suit.

'Ladies and gentlemen,' he said in a voice like warm margarine. Then he paused to grin at everyone. 'It is my immense honour to welcome you tonight to the grand re-  opening of the Squealing Pig. So far the world has only had a taste, a first taste of what is, by all accounts, the most delectable, the most delicious, the most extraordinary, the most incredible-tasting edible in all the world!'

There were huge cheers and applause.

'Who wants some more?'

There were shouts of 'Me! I do! Me! Me!'

Lard raised his hands to silence them.

'Well, I've news for you, ladies and gentle-men. Tonight you shall have *as much as you can eat!*'

And the crowd went wild.

In the kitchens the cooks were rushing about frantically. They had made vast quantities of the recipe and were spooning it at the double on to plates which had been polished up to a sparkle by Madeleine. The waiters were waiting anxiously, shouting for the cooks to hurry up.

A fight nearly broke out between one of the waiters and the Head Chef. It was the whippet-thin waiter who also acted as Lard's spy.

'If he shouts one more time,' whispered the Head Chef, 'I'll chuck him in the deep-fat fryer!'

'Don't bother,' Madeleine whispered back. 'Listen, I've got a plan.' And she told him about the secret recipe she had prepared and how they were to serve it for the second course.

Next door, Paris's richest and most powerful were banging their cutlery on the tables, and when they saw the waiters marching out of the kitchen they

 began to whoop like monkeys. They pounced on the food, saliva dribbling from their chins, and for a while there was no sound but for the busy scraping of metal on china plates.

Monsieur Lard first knew there was something wrong when he saw that people had stopped eating – not the way they had done when they first tasted the delicacy from Madame Pamplemousse's shop. Then they had stopped eating out of awe and wonder. This time they were frowning.

Lard's beady little eyes darted rapidly about the tables and he saw the President of France chewing slowly with a terrible furrowed brow and a man at another table with a napkin over his mouth. A woman was puckering her lips as if she was about to be sick, and then he saw the President stop chewing and suddenly spit violently on to the table. All at once, everyone was coughing, spitting, spluttering, as if they had been poisoned.

Lard leapt up, waving his arms around. 'Wait!' he cried. 'Stop! There must be some mistake. Everyone stop spitting this instant!'

And so they did, not because he told them to but because just then the restaurant doors flew open and out came a solemn procession of cooks, all dressed in their aprons and white hats. And at the front there was the Head Chef, bearing in his hand a tiny plate. This he delivered to the President. 'Monsieur,' he said, 'please accept this from the kitchen, with our apologies.'

The President grunted and, as the crowd watched, he lifted up a tiny spoonful of the food to his mouth. Then he ate another spoonful, and then another. The cooks delivered plates to other tables and soon everyone was doing the same, for Madeleine's recipe had the most incredible effect. It was so deliciously light, so fresh and zingy that people quite forgot their sickness and were soon calling out for more.

On seeing this extraordinary turn of events, Lard got out from under the tablecloth where he had been hiding and dusted himself down.

He had no idea what was going on but assumed the cooks had made a mistake with the first batch of the recipe. He was going to flambé whoever was responsible but, meanwhile, he improvised.

'Ladies and gentlemen,' he grinned broadly, 'as you have probably guessed, that first course you received was really a test! A test to see whether you are truly the finest gourmets in Paris!'

A small murmur of approval went round the tables.

'And you have passed that test! Admirably! You are not only the finest gourmets but also Paris's best and

most beautiful people!'

There was an even bigger murmur of approval. But while he was speaking, a black limousine had slid silently up to the pavement in front of the restaurant. A chauffeur got out to open the passenger door and out stepped the black-suited figure of Monsieur Langoustine. All eyes were on him as he walked up to Monsieur Lard.

'Well, well, nice of you to drop by, Monsieur Langoustine,' said Lard coolly. 'To what do we owe the pleasure?'

'The pleasure is all mine, Monsieur,' said Langoustine. 'For tonight I am here to cele-brate Paris's new gastronomic star.' From out of his long black coat he produced a large bouquet of flowers. 'May I present my compliments to the chef?'

'Really, Monsieur Langoustine,' said Lard, softening like rancid butter, 'you shouldn't have. Though, of course, I accept. For it is an honour and a privilege to be at last recognised as the greatest chef the world has ever –'

Monsieur Langoustine loudly cleared his throat. This was a disturbingly high-pitched, barely human kind of sound, which had the effect of immediately silencing Monsieur Lard. 'Perhaps you didn't hear me correctly, Monsieur,' said Langoustine icily. 'I said I was here to pay my compliments *to the chef*.' He had raised his voice so that all might hear it, although this was unnecessary, since everyone was listening intently. And then he pointed his black-gloved hand in Madeleine's direction. She had been standing in a huddle with the other chefs but, receiving his summons, she stepped out from among them and Monsieur Langoustine presented her with the flowers.

Attached to them was a note, written in exquisite purple script, which read:

For Madeleine, from her friend and colleague, Madame Pamplemousse 🐾

Next to her name there was what appeared to be a smudge of ink, but when Madeleine looked closer she saw it was the tiny imprint of a paw.

'Congratulations, Mademoiselle,' said Langoustine in his soft, piping voice. 'People like us should stick together.' And then he raised her hand to his thin red lips.

A camera flash went off. A photographer had caught the moment and the next day the picture would appear on the cover of every national newspaper: Madeleine in her chef's whites, holding a bunch of bril-liantly coloured flowers, beside a rather sinister-looking man in dark glasses. Above it the headlines would read:

LANGOUSTINE CONGRATULATES NEW GASTRONOMIC STAR

RESTAURANT OWNER STEALS
RECIPE FROM HIS OWN NIECE

MONSIEUR LARD: THIEF!

And in the later editions:

THE MOST INCREDIBLE EDIBLE EVER
TASTED: WAS IT REALLY ALL
A HOAX?

The photographer had also managed to get Monsieur Lard in the picture, his face bright pink, dripping with sweat. As far as situations in which to be unmasked as a thief go, this was arguably the worst. He had personally seen to it that every exit was either fenced off or patrolled by men with guns. His every facial gesture was being broadcast on national television and he was surrounded by a large angry mob who might easily tear him to pieces.

But what they actually did was applaud. No one jeered, no one heckled or booed or hissed. They just stood up and clapped as if the whole thing had been a theatrical event, an entertainment and nothing more.

Then someone called out Madeleine's name and a small tussle broke out among the press, trying to get the first interview. Paris's top children's clothing designer was there, trying to get her to model a new kind of pink fairy outfit with elasticated wings. But no one could find her.

During all the commotion, while everyone's attention had been diverted by the flashing lights of the cameras, Monsieur Langoustine and Madeleine had discreetly made their way through the crowd. And when they reached the limousine, the chauffeur got out to open the door and together they slipped inside. And if anyone had been looking they might have been surprised to see the driver of the car was not even human, but a cat: a long white cat walking on its hind legs and wearing a peaked cap. But no one did notice and before they would have had the chance, the car had already started and was moving silently away.

Epilogue

Madeleine no longer washes dishes in the Squealing Pig. Monsieur Lard sold the restaurant to the Head Chef and his wife, who changed the name to the Hungry Snail, and ever since have made it a big success.

 They also asked Madeleine if she would like to come and live with them. Madeleine's parents agreed, provided they were financially reimbursed for the loss of their child.

Monsieur Lard left Paris and now drives a van, selling chips on the sea coast – and rumour has it they're not bad at all.

But whenever she can, Madeleine goes to visit two friends of hers who run a shop. A small, rather shabby-looking shop. And as the sun sets you will often find them talking and laughing together on a balcony, high above the rooftops of Paris.

In the streets of lebanon
on the banks of the
[illegible]

3 girls
4 boys
all d...
the girl ... they
W...
N... he ...
no ... th... k
like that
all ... line
fr...
...
While ... the ...
As the ...
for new adventures,
wonders, and beliefs /